No Carrots For Harry!

A Parents Magazine
Read Aloud Original

No Carrots For Harry!

by Jean Langerman
pictures by Frank Remkiewicz

PARENTS MAGAZINE PRESS
NEW YORK

Library of Congress Cataloging-in-Publication Data
Langerman, Jean.
No carrots for Harry/by Jean Langerman; pictures
by Frank Remkiewicz.
p. cm.
Summary: Harry the rabbit is adamant about not eating
carrots until he goes to Aunt Prue's for dinner.
ISBN: 0-8193-1190-1
[1. Rabbits—Fiction. 2. Carrots—Fiction.]
I. Remkiewicz, Frank, ill. II. Title.
PZ7.L2625Rab 1989
[E]—dc20 89-3373
CIP
AC

Printed in the United States of America.
10 9 8 7 6 5 4 3 2

To Ross—J.L.

For my uncle, Ed Hyjek,
who got me started drawing rabbits—F.R.

Harry never ate carrots.
If he was offered a carrot at breakfast,
he would politely say, "No, thank you."
If he was offered a carrot at lunch,
he would say, "I never eat carrots."
If he was offered a carrot at dinner,
he would cry, "Yecch! I *hate* carrots!"

No, Harry did *not* like carrots.
But he LOVED sweetgrass tarts.

One day, Harry's family was invited
to Aunt Prue's house for dinner.
Just before Papa Rabbit
knocked at the door, he said,
"Children, mind whatever Aunt Prue says."
Harry and his brothers and sisters
promised, "Yes, Papa."

Then Mama Rabbit said,
"And remember, children,
you must eat what is set before you.
All of it!"
Harry could smell sweetgrass tarts baking.
So along with his brothers and sisters,
he promised, "Yes, Mama."

While they played before dinner,
all Harry could think about was
the taste of sweetgrass tarts.
But he had to eat dinner before dessert.
He hoped he would like it.
"Dinner is ready!" called Aunt Prue.

Harry looked at his plate.

There, with the fine cabbage leaves,
and the sweet green peas,
and the lacy parsley,
sat a big, fat, crisp, orange CARROT!

Oh, *no*!

Harry nibbled through the cabbage leaves.
When they were gone,
the carrot seemed larger.
It was crouched next to the peas,
waiting.

Harry ate the sweet green peas
one by one,
slowly,
until they were gone.
The carrot,
which had grown much larger,
hunched its huge shoulders
against the lacy parsley.

"My carrot keeps growing!"
Harry whispered to his mother.

"No whispering at the table,"
scolded Aunt Prue.
"Sorry," said Harry.

He picked up the dainty
sprig of parsley
and chewed each tiny leaf cluster
as he watched the carrot
slowly growing larger.

All around the table,
the other plates were empty.
Everyone was waiting
for Harry to eat the carrot.

He tried to smile at Aunt Prue.
"No sweetgrass tarts
for naughty little rabbits
who don't eat their carrots,"
Aunt Prue said.

Harry's whiskers quivered.
His ears wilted sadly.
NO SWEETGRASS TARTS?

Aunt Prue went to the kitchen.
She brought back a large plate
filled with tarts.
She passed a tart to each rabbit—
except Harry.

As Harry watched all the others
eating sweetgrass tarts,
he became very angry.
"It's all *your* fault!"
he yelled at the carrot.
Everyone around the table stared.

Harry snatched the carrot
off his plate and snapped it in half.
Then, because he was still so angry,
he bit the carrot—*hard*.

Juice trickled down his chin.
He put out his tongue to lick it off.

"Hmm," said Harry.
"Carrots taste good!"
And he took another bite.

Aunt Prue smiled and said,
"Save the last tart for Harry!"

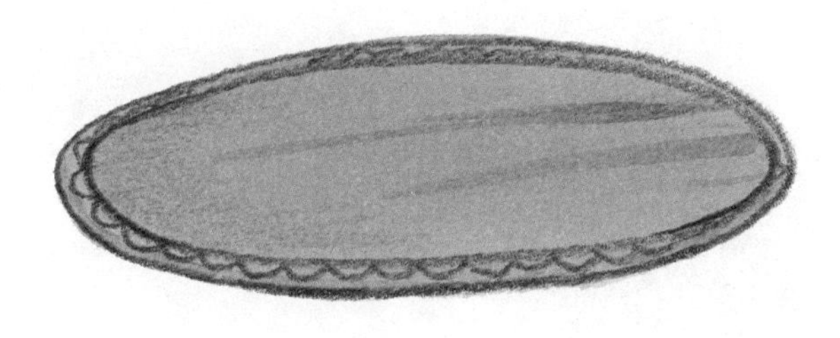

About the Author

Jean Langerman remembers a very unusual wild rabbit that came out of the woods near her house one day. "My husband, Ross, offered the rabbit some pieces of carrot. The rabbit stood with its front paws on Ross' knee, waiting patiently for each slice." As Ms. Langerman watched, she wondered if there had ever been a rabbit that *didn't* like carrots...and quickly created Harry.

Ms. Langerman lives with her husband on twenty-two wooded acres in California.

About the Artist

Frank Remkiewicz remembers visiting a zoo when he was ten. "Afterwards, I wanted to draw a picture of each animal I had seen. I did my first rabbit drawing then—but of course it was nothing like Harry!"

Mr. Remkiewicz has illustrated several children's books, as well as posters, hundreds of greeting cards, and a well-known box of animal crackers. He lives in California with his wife and three daughters.